Earth Geeks Must Go!

Look for more books in the Goosebumps Series 2000
by R.L. Stine:

Earth Geeks Must Go!

AN
APPLE
PAPERBACK

SCHOLASTIC INC.
New York Toronto London Auckland
Sydney New Delhi Hong Kong

A PARACHUTE PRESS BOOK

ISBN-13: 978-0-590-68537-5

This edition is for sale in Indian subcontinent only.

First Scholastic printing, December 1999
Reprinted by Scholastic India Pvt. Ltd., September 2007
March 2008; January; August 2010; May 2011; January 2012
July; December 2013; September; December 2014; July 2015

Printed at Magic International, Greater Noida

My name is Jacob Miller, and I'm a normal guy.

At least, I've always thought of myself as a normal guy, with a normal family and normal friends. My life has never been exciting or special.

I guess you might say there's nothing special about me, either. I'm about average height for a sixth grader, and average weight. I guess I look okay. I have short dark hair and brown eyes. And some people say I have a nice smile.

I'm interested in normal things. I'm into sports. I play soccer and softball. I'm a pretty good swimmer. I like action movies, and I like to read books about baseball and about people who have wild adventures. You know. Like people who spend six months in a raft on the ocean, or people who climb Mount Everest and barely survive.

I get pretty good grades — not perfect, but mostly A's and B's. I guess if I worked harder, I could be a better student. But I'm pretty happy the way I am.

I have a few really good friends. They are nice, normal guys, and when we hang out after school or on weekends, we just mess around or go to the movies at the mall. Ordinary things.

I don't have much of a temper. I almost never get depressed or angry or down on myself. Mom and Dad say I'm "easygoing," whatever that means.

I guess you get the picture.

I'm a normal guy.

Totally normal.

So why has my life suddenly turned so weird? Why has everything turned upside down and inside out?

Why does my life depend on a guy everyone calls Crazy Old Phil?

Why isn't my life normal anymore?

Can *anyone* explain what's happening?

Maybe I'd better begin at the beginning. . . .

'm sitting in my new classroom at school.
It's the first day of school.

It *feels* like the first day of school.

Lots of nervous chatter. Giggles and shrill laughter.

It *sounds* like the first day of school.

Chairs scraping. Lockers slamming. Kids shouting and greeting each other. Everyone asking questions — a million questions as they try to find their new classrooms, try to figure out where to go and where to sit.

I'm feeling nervous too, very jittery, a heavy feeling in my stomach. That feeling is weird for me because I'm usually pretty calm, even on a first day of school.

I'm sitting at a desk in the third row, on the

aisle. I'm staring at a stack of books on my desk-top. Textbooks. Very shiny and new.

I open the top one, and it crackles. It's never been opened before. It has that new book smell.

The teacher enters. He's a short, stubby man with a thick nest of red hair on top of a thin, serious face. His eyeglasses have heavy, square black frames. He's wearing baggy brown trousers and a short-sleeved white shirt that shows off his pudgy pink arms.

He leans forward as he walks, as if leaning into a stiff breeze. His red hair appears to fly behind his bobbing head. His expression is stern, solemn.

He doesn't look at the kids settling into their seats, still laughing and talking. He stomps up to his small gray desk in the front of the room and drops a stack of papers on top of it. Then he pulls off the heavy black eyeglasses and wipes them with a handkerchief.

The bell rings loudly. An electronic buzz that echoes off the tall windows along the side of the room.

A few kids keep talking. Others quiet down and turn to face the teacher.

"I'm Mr. Kray," he announces. His voice is deep. A surprising voice. It's the voice of a much taller person.

I still feel nervous, jittery. I glance around.

I focus on the kids around me.

Whoa. Hey — wait a minute.

4

My eyes dart from face to face.

I have a cold feeling at the back of my neck.

Who *are* these kids?

How come I don't recognize any of them?

Every year, there are several new kids in the school. But I know that at least a few of my friends should be here. The school has only two sixth-grade classes.

All of my friends can't be in the other class. That's impossible.

And these kids can't all be new to the school. But I keep going from face to face — and they are strangers, all strangers!

Am I in the wrong room?

Panic sends another chill down my back. I pull my class assignment card from my pocket: JACOB MILLER. MR. KRAY'S 6TH GRADE.

No. I'm in the right room.

That's a relief. I don't have to get up in front of all these kids and say, "Excuse me. I'm in the wrong room."

That would be too embarrassing. Too geeky for words.

So why don't I recognize any of these kids? Not one.

I gaze down the row at a girl with straight blond hair. She's very pretty. Sunlight through the window makes her hair glow like gold. She has her head down. She seems to be scribbling a note to somebody.

Next to her, a tall, athletic-looking boy with a red baseball cap turned sideways on his head grins at me.

Do I know him? Is he grinning at the kid next to me?

I twist around in my seat and check out the kids in the back rows. Do I know any of them? It would sure be nice to see a familiar face.

But, no. They're all strangers too.

"Welcome back to school," Mr. Kray booms. He stands behind the short desk, leaning forward, his fists on the desktop.

I chuckle to myself. He looks a little like a gorilla, leaning over like that. A red-haired gorilla.

"I hope you had a good summer," he continues. Behind the glasses, his eyes move from face to face. "And I hope you're ready to settle down and begin the trelth grade."

The *what*?

What grade?

I raise my hand. "What did you say?" I ask. "What grade?"

A boy in the front row chokes on his chewing gum or something. He coughs and sputters and drowns out my question.

I see a few kids turn to look at me. But Mr. Kray is busy slapping the choking kid on the back.

"I can see you're all choked up to be back in school," the teacher jokes.

A few kids laugh. Most don't.

The boy's face is as red as a tomato, but he's fine. He drops back in his chair, embarrassed, and pretends to study the floor.

I realize I'm gripping the sides of my desk tightly with both hands. I loosen my grip, let out a long breath, and try to relax.

Why am I so stressed out?

Jacob, there's nothing to worry about, I tell myself.

Mr. Kray turns and starts writing on the chalk-board. The chalk squeaks, making a lot of kids cry out. He writes rapidly, making short stabs with the chalk, which squeaks with each stab.

What is he writing?

I lean forward and squint between the two kids in front of me.

Wait a minute. Wait . . . wait . . .

I can't read any of it.

Is he writing in a foreign alphabet? It all looks like crazy squiggles to me.

Is he making up a new language or something? Is this some kind of game?

I blink several times, thinking maybe I can get the squiggles into focus. Get them to make sense.

But I really can't tell if Mr. Kray is writing letters or numbers.

My heart is racing. I can feel the blood pulsing at my temples. That heavy knot in my stomach grows tighter.

I turn to check out the other kids. They all seem to be reading the chalkboard. Some of them are copying it into their notebooks.

How come they can read the strange scrawls and I can't?

Mr. Kray stops. He erases the last section he wrote. He checks a paper on his desk, turns back to the board, and starts scribbling again.

SQUEAK SQUEAK.

The squeak of the chalk sends shiver after shiver down my back.

Why can't I read what he is writing?

Am I *dreaming* this?

Yes. That's the only explanation, I decide.

This is a dream.

I pinch myself. Just like in cartoons. I pinch the back of my hand really hard.

It hurts. I don't wake up.

I'm not dreaming.

I still can't read a thing on the board.

Mr. Kray stops writing and turns around. He brushes chalk dust off the front of his shirt with a chubby pink hand. He glances down at a paper on his desk. Then he turns to us.

He stares directly at me. "Jacob Miller," he says in his deep, ringing voice. "Would you please come up here and solve this for us?"

loud *GULP* escapes my throat.

I can feel my face turning red.

I stare one more time at the strange letters and numbers, praying they will come into focus.

"Please —" Mr. Kray holds out the chalk. "Finish the equation for us, Jacob."

"Uh . . . Well . . ." My whole body is trembling.

The first day of school, and all these new kids are going to think I'm an idiot.

"I can't do that one," I say, trying to keep my voice from cracking. "We didn't study that in Mrs. Palmer's class."

"Who?" a girl whispers somewhere behind me.

A few kids laugh. I see that the pretty girl with the shiny blond hair is eyeing me curiously.

"Anybody?" Mr. Kray swings the chalk in a

wide gesture. "Does anybody want to solve it? I thought we'd start with an easy one."

An easy one? Is he kidding?

An easy one would be in real numbers!

A girl in the front row with curly brown hair raises her hand. She takes the chalk from the teacher, steps up to the board, and starts writing funny squiggles under Mr. Kray's squiggles.

She writes three lines of squiggles, then hands the chalk back to him.

Mr. Kray nods, and a smile crosses his solemn, round face. "Very good, Myrna." He glances at me and his smile fades.

I see other kids looking at me.

I feel myself blushing.

What's wrong with me? I wonder. Should I know how to read that problem?

Did he really say *trelth* grade?

Did I just hear him wrong?

I'm so busy thinking about how strange everything is, I don't hear what Mr. Kray is talking about.

Suddenly, all the kids are jumping up. They climb out of their seats and go to the computers lined up on the counter against the back wall.

"I know it's a boring topic," Mr. Kray says. "But write it anyway. It's a good warm-up practice."

Write what?

I didn't hear the assignment.

I climb up unsteadily. My legs are trembling.

I'm not getting off to a good start, I realize.

Pull yourself together, Jacob, I order myself.

I usually don't have such a hard time. I usually get right into things.

I've been looking forward to school starting for weeks. So why are things going so badly?

I accidentally bite my tongue as I make my way to the last free computer at the end of the table. "Ouch!" I cry out.

A few kids turn away from their computers to stare at me. I pretend I don't see them.

It really hurts when you bite your tongue. My whole mouth is stinging as I sit down at the computer.

I turn to the boy next to me. He is already bent over the keyboard, typing away with both hands. "What are we supposed to write?" I whisper.

He doesn't lower his hands from the keyboard. He turns to me. "The most exciting thing that happened to you last summer," he says. He sighs. "The same old thing every year. Can't they think up anything new?"

I chuckle. "What if you had a really boring summer?"

But he has already started typing away again, staring into the white glow of the monitor.

I turn to my screen. I try to think of something exciting that happened to me last summer. I can't think of a single thing.

Think, Jacob — think!

I glance down at the keyboard — and nearly fall off the chair!

The letters . . . The letters on the keys . . .

I don't recognize them.

They're in an alphabet I've never seen before.

Triangles and curly lines and rows of big and little dots.

I stare at the keys. My mouth hangs open. I suddenly have trouble breathing.

The other kids type away.

I gasp when I feel a hand squeeze my shoulder.

I turn to find Mr. Kray behind me. He glances at my empty monitor screen, then frowns at me. "Having a problem, Jacob?" he asks softly.

"Uh . . . yeah," I choke out. "I . . . uh . . ."

"Can't think of anything to write about?" he asks. "Did you go on a family vacation this summer?"

I nod. "Yes, we did. But —"

"Where did you go?" he asks.

Before I can answer, he reaches over my head and pulls down a large wall map. "Show me where you traveled, Jacob."

I raise my eyes to the map.

"Oh, no . . ."

What kind of a map is this?

None of the countries look familiar. Where is North America? Where is South America? Europe?

So many oceans . . .

Is the map sideways? I tilt my head. No. That doesn't help.

This map can't be right. It's not like any map I've ever seen before.

Mr. Kray narrows his eyes at me behind the black-framed glasses. "What's wrong, Jacob?"

Should I tell him?

Should I tell him the problems I'm having?

Will he understand? Or will he think I'm totally messed up?

Finally, I blurt it out. "Mr. Kray, I think I'm going crazy. Nothing is right."

The bell rings. Right above my head. I jump a mile.

"Lunch, everyone!" Mr. Kray calls. "I'll see you back here after lunch."

The scrape of chairs. Laughter. Loud voices.

Mr. Kray didn't hear me. He turns and walks back to his desk.

I stand up, feeling shaky, in a daze. I have that light-headed feeling I sometimes get after swimming for a long time.

I take one last glance at the strange squiggles on the chalkboard. Then I wander into the hall.

What is happening to me? I wonder.

Will anyone help me figure this out?

don't feel hungry. But I grab the paper bag containing my lunch and make my way to the lunchroom.

As I walk down the long halls, I realize they don't look familiar. Were the walls always green? Where are the lockers? Didn't the music room used to be next to the language lab?

I know I'm in the right school. There's no way I could have wandered into the wrong building. But why does it look so different today?

In the lunchroom, I search desperately for my friends. But I can't find them.

Other kids are laughing and talking happily. They seem to know each other.

But they are all strangers to me.

I can't find a familiar face in the lunchroom, either.

I sit at a table near the back. I stare at my lunch bag without opening it.

At the next table, three girls in cheerleader uniforms are singing a song I don't recognize. Across from me two guys are trading lunches.

I keep picturing the weird map — all those strange countries and oceans. And I think about the keyboard with the weird, foreign alphabet on it.

My stomach growls. I decide I'd better eat.

I pull the sandwich from the bag and unwrap it. Some kind of lunch meat. Not very appetizing.

But I pick up a sandwich half and raise it to my mouth. I'm about to take a bite — when I see several kids staring at me. Such startled expressions on their faces!

I lower the sandwich half to the table and glance around from table to table.

Hey — what is going on?

To my shock, the kids have all pushed up their shirtsleeves.

And they are stuffing food into their ARM-PITS!

I blink. And blink again.

This isn't happening.

It can't be.

I try not to look at them. Instead, I raise the sandwich half to my mouth again.

"Oooh, gross!" I hear a girl exclaim.

Once again, I lower the sandwich half. My heart is pounding. I start to feel sick.

Two girls at the end of my table are staring at me in disgust. "Were you really going to put that sandwich in your *mouth*?" one of them asks.

"Yuck," the other one adds. "Totally gross."

I force a smile to my face. It isn't easy. I feel like puking. Or hiding. "Uh . . . just joking," I manage to say. "Ha-ha. Dumb, huh?"

"Just gross," one of them replies, making a face. "Why do guys think it's such a riot to be gross?"

17

The girls go back to their lunches. They raise their arms, and I can see big holes in their armpits. And pointed white teeth going in a circle inside the holes.

One girl shoves an apple into her armpit hole.

I hear horrible chewing sounds.

Now I *really* feel sick!

Her friend shoves a bunch of grapes into her armpit. *SQUISH SQUISH.*

All around the room, kids have their sleeves up, and they are pushing food into their armpits.

A chubby boy in a bright yellow T-shirt is dumping a container of yogurt into his armpit. A boy across from him holds a milk carton with the straw poking into his armpit. The armpit tightens around the straw, and I hear loud slurping sounds as it drinks.

At a table near the window, a boy is feeding potato chips to a girl. He slides them one by one into her armpit. They laugh and talk as they eat.

Some boys have taken their shirts off completely and sit bare-chested at the table. One boy is eating with two hands, shoving food into both armpits. Kids laugh and point at him.

"Piggy! Piggy!" Someone starts a chant, and several other kids pick it up. The boy doesn't seem to mind. He keeps shoving tuna salad into both pits.

I swallow hard to keep from gagging.

At the next table, I see a girl watching me. She

has dark eyes and dark brown hair cut very short and straight, with a row of bangs across her forehead.

Why is she staring at me like that? I wonder. Does she suspect that I'm different?

Does she think I'm weird because I haven't pulled my shirt down? Because I'm not stuffing my lunch into my armpit?

Suddenly, I realize I don't want kids to know. I don't want them to see that I am different.

Not until I figure it all out.

I turn away from the girl. I shove my lunch away and jump to my feet.

I can't take it anymore.

I'm going crazy. That's the only answer.

I've lost my mind. I'm a total crazy person.

My chair falls over as I lurch away from the table. I see kids staring at me, but I don't care.

I start to run. My legs are shaky. My stomach heaves.

I clap a hand over my mouth and keep running.

As if in a dream, I see faces floating all around, faces watching me, staring at me as I run.

I see arms raised high. Open armpits. Chewing armpits.

Chewing . . . chewing . . .

I lurch into the hall, still holding my hand over my mouth. I turn the corner and nearly run into two teachers, chatting, slapping each other's shoulders.

19

They stop when I run past. "Hey —" one of them calls out.

But I keep running, my shoes slapping the hard floor.

I reach the back of the school building and shove the door open with both hands.

I'm out in the fresh air now. A sunny, warm day that feels more like summer than fall.

I keep running. Across the teacher parking lot. Over the practice field.

Into the woods behind the school grounds.

I push my way blindly through weeds and bushes, between the tangle of old trees. I've got to get away from there. Got to find a place where I can think. Where I can try to figure this out.

I make my way through a clump of tall reeds, creaking and bending in the soft wind. On the other side of the reeds, I stop to catch my breath.

And hear the scrape of footsteps behind me.

And realize I'm being followed.

ho is chasing after me?

Teachers?

Kids who have figured out that I'm not like them, that I don't belong?

What do they want?

Why are they chasing me?

My heart pounding, I turn and try to peer through the tall reeds.

But they're too thick. I can't see.

The footsteps are rapid and steady. Just on the other side of the reeds now.

I suck in a deep breath — and take off.

My shoes slip on soft dirt.

My side aches from running.

I turn sharply, into a line of pine trees. I duck under low branches, holding my arms out like a shield.

I stumble over a blanket of pinecones.

My feet slide out from under me.

I start to fall. "Whoa!" I grab the rough, gnarled trunk of a tree.

And hear the steady footsteps coming. Closer . . . Closer . . .

Past the pine trees, I see a low mound of gray stones. I dive behind them and listen.

The pine trees shake as someone hurtles through them, moving fast.

I need to find a better place to hide.

But where?

I spot a field of tall grass, crackling and bending in the wind.

The crunch of footsteps comes closer.

I lower my head and run frantically into the tall grass. Into the cool, dark safety of the grass.

Panting like an animal, I lower my hands to my knees and struggle to catch my breath.

I listen for the footsteps.

Silence now.

The *CAW* of a bird in a nearby tree. The whisper of the wind through the grass.

But no sound of shoes pounding the ground.

I did it!

I lost whoever was chasing me.

But something is wrong.

My legs suddenly itch.

I bend. Pull up my jeans to scratch.

And gasp in horror.

I gape at the insects up and down my legs.

Stuck to my skin. Attached to me.

Fat, round insects. Dozens of them. Clinging to my legs. Up to my knees.

Faceless insects. Legless.

"Ohhhh." A sick groan escapes my mouth. They look like bubbles, bubbles the size of quarters — bubbles covered with spiky black hair.

I stare at them. They pulse and quiver.

They make low grunting sounds. Like pigs at the trough.

They're drinking my blood!

I grab at one. Squeeze it between my fingers. And pull.

Its hair is sticky and wet. It makes a *SQUISH* as I try to tug it off my skin.

It won't budge!

I tug harder.

My legs throb and itch! The itching spreads up my whole body.

I can't help it. I open my mouth — and scream.

A shrill scream of horror.

Then I bend over and tug at the sticky, bubbly bugs with both hands. Tug frantically.

They loosen with a sick sucking sound.

I toss them wildly into the trees.

My chest heaving, the trees spinning in front of my dazed eyes, I work frantically.

Only a few left now. I pull one off my knee and heave it to the dirt. It makes a sick *SPLAT* as it hits.

And then I take off.

My legs still itching, my whole body prickling, I run through the trees.

Toward the school? Away from the school?

I don't know. I've lost all sense of direction now.

I'm just running. Trying to escape the sight of those fat, hair-covered bugs. Trying to escape the feel of them stuck to my skin.

I run . . . run away from everything that happened to me that morning, the first morning at school.

And I run right into my pursuer.

We collide. My lowered head hits her shoulder. Her arms fly up.

The force of our collision sends her sprawling to the ground.

We both cry out.

I fall beside her on the grass.

She jumps to her feet first. She brushes off the back of her red-and-white tank top and her black jeans.

She stands over me.

I scramble to my feet.

"Hey!" I cry out as I recognize her.

The girl from the lunchroom. The girl with the short dark brown hair who had been studying me so intently.

Her eyes narrow coldly. "I've been watching you, Jacob."

I glance quickly from side to side, searching for an escape route. "Why?" I shout. "What do you want? What do you *want*?"

She shakes her head to straighten her short dark brown bangs. Her dark eyes burn into mine.

"I — I don't know what I want," she stammers. She lets out a long sigh.

A stab of pain makes me cry out. I pull up a jeans leg and find another fat, hairy bug attached to my ankle. With a groan, I tug it off and toss it away.

I turn back to the girl. "What's your name? Why did you follow me? Why were you watching me?"

"Calm down," she says sharply. "I'm not going to hurt you. Why are you so afraid?"

"Because," I answer. Brilliant. "I have a lot of reasons," I add.

"My name is Arlene," she says.

"Answer the rest of my questions," I say. "Why were you watching me?"

"Because you're different from the others," she replies.

She's found me out, I realize. I'm caught.

"And I'm different too," she continues. "I'm like you, Jacob."

Is she lying?

Is she trying to trick me?

I cross my arms over my chest. My T-shirt is soaked with sweat. "Prove it," I say. "Prove you're like me."

She doesn't hesitate. "Okay. Look." She pushes up the sleeve of her sweater. She raises her arm.

No food hole in her armpit.

"I'm not like them," Arlene says softly, still holding her arm above her head. "I eat with my mouth. Like you."

I still don't trust her. "Maybe I don't eat with my mouth," I say. "Maybe I think that's gross and disgusting."

"I saw you," she insists. "You started to put that sandwich in your mouth, but that girl stopped you."

I shove my hands into my jeans pockets. "I haven't seen you in school before, Arlene. Where are you from?" I ask.

She lowers her eyes to the ground. "I — I don't remember." She says it in a whisper.

I stare hard at her. "You're kidding, right? You *have* to remember where you're from."

"N-no," she stammers. She raises her eyes to me. I see tears glisten in them. "I really don't remember. I don't even remember my last name."

"Huh?" I continue to stare at her.

A tear rolls down her cheek. "Are you from here?" she asks, wiping it away with one finger.

"I — I —" My mouth drops open. I can't remember where I'm from.

What's going on?

Why can't I remember where I'm from?

"I — I don't know, either," I say.

My legs are trembling too hard to hold me. I suddenly feel so dizzy. I drop down onto the grass. I lean my back against a tree trunk.

And shut my eyes, trying to remember.

Where do I live? Where do I come from?

Why can't I remember?

"It's so frightening," Arlene says. "I don't know any of the kids in this school. And I can't read their language."

"Me, neither," I whisper.

"But I came to school the normal way this morning," she continues. "Everything seemed the same. But then the school was totally different. The teachers were all different, and so were the kids. And — and —" The words catch in her throat.

"Do you think we're the only two?" I ask.

28

Before she can answer, I hear a loud *SPLAT*.

Arlene lets out a shriek. She grabs at her hair. She pulls off a fat, hairy bug. "Yuck. What *is* this?"

"They're horrible bugs. They —"

That's all I get out.

Another *SPLAT*. A hairy bubble lands on my shoulder. Another one *SPLATS* onto my head.

I tug at it. It's attached to my hair. Another one rolls down my back. Another . . .

The tree is raining bugs.

The bugs attach to my hair, my forehead, my cheeks, down my back.

They're grunting . . . pulsing . . . quivering over my skin.

Arlene slaps at them. Pulls them from her hair with both hands.

She opens her mouth to scream — and a hairy bug drops onto her tongue.

She slaps it away, gagging and choking.

Too many of them. Too many . . .

They are covering us . . . drowning us. Grunting and sucking, sticking to our faces, our backs, our chests . . .

We both scream. Scream at the top of our lungs.

"Help us! Somebody — please! Help us!"

10

hear voices. Shouts. The thud of running feet.

Kids appear, five or six of them, red-faced from running, their hair blowing wild. I recognize the girl named Myrna and the boy from my class with the red baseball cap.

They circle us quickly.

Arlene and I are slapping at the bugs, pulling them from our hair, our skin.

"Splatters!" Myrna says.

"Splatters!" other kids repeat.

That's what these disgusting bugs are called, I realize. Splatters.

"Help us —" Arlene pleads.

"What can we do?" I ask, ripping a Splatter from my eyebrow. "Help!"

Myrna brushes a hairy bug from the shoulder of

her green T-shirt. She puckers her lips and begins to whistle.

The other kids start to whistle. High, shrill notes. Not musical. I realize they are whistling as loudly as they can.

The bugs up and down my arms tremble and shake. I stare at them helplessly, watching them quiver. I can feel bugs quivering in my hair.

I see a Splatter fall off Arlene's shoulder. Another bug drops from her forehead.

Taking deep breaths, the kids whistle louder, higher.

The sound is so shrill, my ears hurt. My head feels about to explode.

Louder . . .

The Splatters quiver, then drop to the ground. They make a pattering *THUD* as they land. It sounds like big raindrops hitting the dirt.

The kids keep whistling till all the bugs have dropped off.

I scratch my head, scratch the back of my neck. The bugs are gone, but my skin still prickles.

"Th-thanks," I stammer.

"Why didn't you whistle?" Myrna asks, eyeing Arlene and me suspiciously. "You know that's the only way to get the Splatters off."

"Everyone knows that," a boy mutters.

"Uh . . . I guess Jacob and I just panicked," Arlene says.

The boy in the red cap reaches down and picks

up one of the hairy, bubble-shaped insects. He slaps it between his hands. It makes a loud *POP*, like a balloon bursting. And a disgusting yellow liquid sprays out.

The boy laughs and picks up another one.

He pops it and sprays the yellow goo on the boy next to him.

This starts a Splatter war. Laughing and shouting, the kids grab up the bugs and pop them between their hands, splattering thick yellow gunk on each other.

Arlene and I exchange glances. Should we join in?

Kids around here obviously splatter these insects for fun.

But I remember how they feel in my hair, attaching to my skin, clinging to my face. I shudder. I really don't want to touch them again.

After a minute or so, the Splatter war ends. I realize the kids are all staring at Arlene and me.

They surround us once again. Their expressions turn serious.

"Why are you out here?" Myrna asks. "You know you're not supposed to come out here during the school day."

"We . . . just wanted to talk," I tell her, glancing nervously at Arlene.

"But you know how dangerous the woods are," a boy says. "You know the rule."

No, we don't, I think. *We don't know anything about this school.*

We don't even know anything about OUR-SELVES.

The kids close in on us, making the circle tighter. A boy steps on a Splatter, and yellow goo oozes around his shoe.

"We heard you shouting, so we came running," the boy in the red cap says.

"But you will get us all in trouble," a girl says softly. "If they see us out here . . ." She lowers her eyes. Her voice trails off.

"We have no choice," Myrna says. "Come with us."

Panic grips my throat. "Huh? Where are you taking us?"

"To the principal," Myrna replies. "To Mr. Trager. We have to explain."

"But —" I start.

"You don't want to get us *all* in trouble on the very first day, do you?" a boy demands.

Arlene and I have no choice. We follow them back to the school building. They lead us to an office near the front entrance.

A man in a gray suit and vest appears. He is about forty, with tanned cheeks, bright blue eyes, and graying hair slicked down and parted in the middle. Mr. Trager.

He leads Arlene and me into the back office and

closes the door. We stand awkwardly in front of his long gray desk.

He studies us for a while, narrowing those glowing blue eyes at us. His hair has so much oil in it, it gleams under the fluorescent lights.

He wasn't the principal here last year, I think.

Miss Robison was the principal. She was the principal forever!

But is this the same school?

Why can't I remember?

Mr. Trager rubs his tanned chin and turns to me. "You were found in the woods?"

I nod. "Yes."

My heart is thudding in my chest. My hands are suddenly ice-cold. I shove them into my jeans pockets.

"You both sneaked into the woods?" the principal asks, turning to Arlene.

She hesitates. "Well . . . yes."

Mr. Trager shakes his head. "You both have committed a fatal crime," he says sternly. "You know the punishment. Do you have any last words?"

My knees start to fold. I grab the desk to keep from falling.

A short cry escapes Arlene's lips.

Mr. Trager tosses his head back and laughs. I can see a mouthful of gold fillings.

"Don't look so serious," he says. He slaps my shoulder. "You know I'm kidding."

Kidding. I let out a sigh. I start to breathe again. He was only kidding.

Great joke.

He frowns at us. "But you both know you're not allowed in the woods during school. What were you doing out there?"

I have a sudden urge to tell him the truth.

We don't know where we come from, Mr. Trager. And we don't know anyone in this school. And we can't read or write your language.

35

That would go over big — wouldn't it?

"We thought we saw some kind of animal in the woods," I lie. "So we followed it. We didn't mean to go so far."

Mr. Trager's blue eyes lock on mine. "There are lots of animals in those woods," he says softly. "That's why we have the rule."

"It's the first day of school. We just forgot," Arlene chimes in.

Mr. Trager drops heavily into his desk chair. It makes a loud *WHOOSH* as he sits down. He taps a pencil on the metal desktop as he gazes up at me.

"Jacob, I also heard you were seen in the lunchroom putting food in your mouth."

I swallow. My throat suddenly feels dry. "Well . . ."

"Don't be so impolite, Jacob," he scolds. "It's not funny. You know that's a disgusting thing to do while people are eating."

"Sorry," I murmur, looking down at the carpet.

But I don't have a food hole in my armpit, I think.

I think shoving food into your armpit is disgusting.

I suddenly wish I could ask him a million questions:

What school is this? What town are we in? What language did Mr. Kray write on the board? Why can't Arlene remember her last name? Why can't I remember where I live?

So many questions . . .

Thinking about them makes me start to shake. I realize for the first time just how frightened I am.

"You'd better get to class now," Mr. Trager says, leading us out of the office. "No more trouble, okay? You are trelth graders now. You have to set a good example."

Trelth?

Arlene and I wander down the hall. Lockers slam. Kids are getting their books and supplies, hurrying to class.

Arlene stops at her locker. She is biting her bottom lip. Her chin quivers. "This is so scary," she whispers.

Then she slaps at her back. "Ow!" She reaches behind her and pulls a hairy Splatter bug from her back. "Ow. Ow. That really hurt. It was burrowing into my skin."

"Give it to me." I take the disgusting bug from her. I place it in my palm and raise my hand to slap it.

Arlene grabs my hand as I bring it down. "Don't," she says.

"What's your problem?" I ask.

"It's a living thing, Jacob. Don't kill it."

"Huh?" I stare at it. The bug grunts. It quivers in my hand, a hair-covered bubble.

"I don't believe in killing living creatures," Arlene says. She shakes her head to straighten her bangs.

Holding the bug in my palm, I turn and walk past the principal's office, down the hall to a side door. I push open the door and carry the bug outside.

I see a low brick wall on the other side of the parking lot. Beyond the wall is the playground.

I carry the bug to the grass and carefully set it down. I am really tempted to stomp on it and make it pop.

But Arlene is watching me from the doorway.

So I turn and start back to the school building.

I take a few steps — and hear a whispered voice. "Hey, kid — over here." From behind the brick wall.

Startled, I turn to see an unpleasant-looking man. A thick stubble of beard on his face. Scraggly black hair falling over his eyes.

"Quick — over here!"

A chill of fear prickles the back of my neck.

Who is he? What does he want?

Why is he hiding back there?

I start to run. I don't feel safe until I'm back in the school and the door is closed behind me.

But am I really safe?

12

The rest of the day goes very slowly. I try to hide behind the kid in front of me. I don't want to be called on because I don't understand anything Mr. Kray is talking about.

He gives us a geography lesson on the continent of Plosia.

Then he assigns us to read the first three chapters in a novel by Thomas Maroon.

I feel lost, totally lost.

My head swims. I struggle to think clearly. But I'm too afraid.

And too hungry. My stomach growls so loudly, the girl next to me laughs. I didn't get to eat any lunch. I realize if I'm ever going to eat, it will have to be in private.

I stare at the clock, but it seems to be moving backwards. And I can't read the strange numbers on it. And why are there fourteen numbers instead of twelve?

I wonder how Arlene is doing. She isn't in my class. She's in the other sixth-grade class. Or should I say, the other *trelth*-grade class?

I feel a stab of fear. What if Arlene is tricking me? What if she really *isn't* different like me? What if she's setting some kind of a trap?

Can I really trust her?

I take a deep breath and hold it. Don't panic, Jacob, I tell myself. Arlene is as frightened as you are. She doesn't have a mouth in her armpit. You can trust her.

You have to trust *someone*.

I breathe a sigh of relief when the bell finally rings.

Everyone hurries out. They are all laughing and joking and happy.

I feel exhausted. Totally stressed. I know I can't spend one more day in this school struggling to hide the fact that I'm different, that I don't belong.

But what can I do?

Arlene is waiting for me at my locker. She looks pale, and her expression is troubled. "We have to talk," she whispers.

I toss my books into the locker and pull out my jacket. "I know," I say. "How did it go this afternoon?"

"A disaster," Arlene replies, her voice trembling. "I couldn't understand a thing. Miss Blinn asked me to read a paragraph in a book out loud. Of course I couldn't read the strange letters."

"What did you do?" I ask.

"I pretended to have a coughing fit." She utters a sigh. "But I can't do that every day!"

We walk past the playground and see kids playing some kind of a sport. Two teams are tossing two silvery disks the size of CDs back and forth. The players catch the disks in big, three-fingered gloves.

There's a lot of cheering and shouting with each catch.

"That's a meener!" a boy is yelling. "Double meener!"

"It's out! It's not a meener!" a girl argues.

"Double meener! That's a do-over!"

"But he stepped on the scrog!"

A big argument stops the game. Two kids toss the disks high above their heads, catching them in their own gloves, waiting for the argument to end.

"It isn't a meener if he steps on the scrog."

"But it's *your* screm!"

"No — the screm changed. It was *your* screm!"

Arlene and I stop for just a moment to watch. I see the boy in the red cap waving to me. "Hey, Jacob! Jacob, you're on our team! Come on!"

"No —" I protest. "I can't."

Because I have no idea how to play your weird game! I think.

"Your friend can play too," the boy calls. "Come on. We're just starting the first drell!"

41

"Sorry," I say. "We have to be somewhere."

Arlene and I cross the street and hurry away. I can still hear their arguing voices.

"That's another meener. You scratch!"

"Toss the krill! Come on, toss the krill!"

As we hurry along the sidewalk, I turn to Arlene and see tears in her eyes. "What are we going to do, Jacob?" she whispers. "This is all so . . . weird."

We walk a few blocks, past pretty square-shaped houses with neatly trimmed front lawns. A dog barks at us from inside a house.

It makes me happy to hear such a normal sound.

We cross another street and enter a small green park. I point to a bench half-hidden by flowering shrubs, and we sit down.

"What are we going to do?" Arlene repeats. She clasps her hands tensely in her lap and chews her bottom lip.

I lean back against the wooden bench. I gaze up at the leafy trees, wondering if there are Splatter bugs up there waiting to rain down.

"Let's try really hard to remember things," I suggest.

Arlene nods. "Okay."

"Try to remember your last name," I say. "Shut your eyes and think really hard."

She does as I say. She's silent for a long time. When she opens her eyes, they are red-rimmed, troubled.

"No," she says. "I can't remember. I'm Arlene. Arlene *blank*. Arlene no-name. It — it's so horrible!"

I squeeze her hand. It's ice-cold.

"Let me see what I can remember," I say. I think hard. And a picture slowly comes into focus in my mind. A picture of a small house.

"I think I remember where I live," I say softly. "I think it's somewhere over there." I point.

"Really?" she cries. "That's great! How long have you lived there? Do you remember?"

I shut my eyes and concentrate. My throat tightens. "No," I say. "I . . . don't remember."

"Have you lived there a long time or a short time, Jacob? Think."

"I really can't remember."

"Do you have any brothers or sisters?"

I shake my head. "I can't remember, Arlene." I start to feel sick. The park starts to spin.

I stand up. "Let's get out of here. Let's try to find the house. Maybe my mom and dad are there. Maybe they can explain what is going on."

Arlene doesn't move from the bench. She gazes up at me sadly. "Do you remember your mom and dad?"

I stare back at her. I try to picture my parents. "No. No, I don't."

"We . . . we're in trouble, Jacob," Arlene says softly.

She climbs to her feet, and we start to walk in

silence. We don't say a word. I guess we're both thinking about our problem, both trying to remember *one thing* about our lives.

The neighborhood doesn't look at all familiar. We stop in front of a small stone building. A sign above the door has a painting of books, dozens of brightly colored books spilling off a shelf.

"Maybe this is a library," I say.

I want to go home. I want to see what Mom and Dad look like.

I want *answers* to all my questions.

But Arlene grabs my arm and yanks me up the library steps. "Let's go in. We can learn something in there. I know we can."

The library is brightly lit and smells fresh and clean. Shelves of books on all sides stretch from floor to ceiling. A black cat sleeps curled up on a shelf beside the front desk.

The librarian is a pretty young woman with straight black hair pulled back in a ponytail and a friendly smile. "Can I help you?" she asks. "I'm Miss Nash. I haven't seen you two here before."

"We're new," Arlene says.

"Do you have books about this place?" I ask.

Miss Nash narrows her eyes at me. "You mean local history?"

I nod. "Yes. And geography, I guess. You know. Maps and stuff."

"Go through that door to the main reading

room." She points to a narrow door behind her. "The last shelf on the right on the back wall."

We thank her and make our way to the door.

"If you have any questions, please ask," the librarian calls.

I have a MILLION questions, I think.

But maybe — just maybe — I'll find some answers right now.

The main reading room is long and narrow. One endless table runs down the middle of the room. Several people are sitting on both sides of the table, leaning over books and newspapers.

Arlene and I squeeze past them and walk to the back wall. We find the last shelf on the right. We don't stop to read titles. We just begin pulling books out.

We both carry armloads of books to the table. Two seats at the very end are empty. We drop down next to each other.

I smile at Arlene across the table. "Now maybe we'll finally find out where we are and what is happening to us."

She leans over my shoulder as I slide the first heavy book off the stack. I pull open the cover. Start to flip through the pages.

And we both gasp in horror.

"We should have known," Arlene whispers.

We stare down at the strange, unreadable alphabet.

Of course. Of course. The books aren't in English.

They aren't in any alphabet we've ever seen before. Not even the same language we saw in school.

I slam the first book shut and try the next. And the next and the next.

One book is filled with maps. None of the countries looks familiar. And we can't read their names because the words are just squiggles.

"It's useless." Arlene sighs.

I run my hand over the page. It's bumpy. The letters stick up from the page like braille.

I turn and gaze down the long table.

People lean over their books. Their eyes are shut. Their heads move from side to side as they run their tongues over the pages.

They're reading the bumpy language with their tongues!

"Arlene — you're right. This is useless," I whisper. "Let's get out of here."

I close the book and start to back away from the table.

But something catches my eye behind a tall bookshelf across from us.

Someone behind the shelf. A man.

He ducks his head when he realizes I've spotted him.

But I recognize him. I recognize the stubbly beard, the hair falling over his eyes.

The scary guy who called to me from behind the playground wall.

Is he following me?

I grab Arlene's arm and tug her to the door. "Hurry. Run."

She hesitates for a moment, and then we both take off.

"Hey —" Miss Nash calls out in surprise as we tear past her.

Out the door. Back onto the street.

I turn back, my heart pounding in my chest.

Is the creepy guy behind us?

Yes.

"**C**ome on!" I cry.

I pull Arlene by the arm. We dart across the street. I hear the sharp blare of a car horn. Hear the squeal of brakes.

But we don't stop to see what nearly hit us.

We run into the little park. I drag Arlene behind the tall, flowering bushes.

"Who — who was that?" she stammers breathlessly.

I'm panting too hard to answer. "I don't know," I finally choke out. "He — he's following me. He tried to get me — at school this morning."

I peek around the side of the bush. I see the man run into the park. He's wearing a stained raincoat. He has a wide-brimmed hat pulled down over his hair.

Shielding his eyes from the late afternoon sun-

48

light with one hand, he turns one way, then the other, searching for us. He makes a complete circle.

Please, I pray silently, *don't come this way.*
Please don't come past these bushes.

The man freezes. And stares straight ahead.

I pull my head back behind the shrub.

"Can you see him? Do you recognize him? Is he coming this way?" Arlene whispers in my ear.

I don't answer. I peek back out.

The man has vanished.

"A close one," I whisper. We wait a few more minutes to make sure he's gone. I realize I'm shaking all over.

"Now what?" Arlene asks.

"Let's go to my house," I say.

Arlene glances nervously around the park. "Will we be safe there?" she asks.

"I don't know," I reply.

The house is long and low. The front is gray shingles with dark green shutters on the window.

We stop at the bottom of the driveway. "How do you know this is your house?" Arlene asks.

I stare at the dark windows, struggling to remember. "I don't know. I just have a feeling."

I make my way up the driveway and peer into the garage through the window on the door. Empty. No car inside.

I lead the way onto the front stoop. The front door is painted green to match the shutters. The door isn't locked. I push it open and we go inside.

"Anybody home?" I call in a timid voice.

Silence. The only sound is the ticking of the tall wooden clock on the mantelpiece.

"Are your mom and dad home this early?" Arlene

asks, looking around the living room tensely. "Does this room look familiar? Do you remember it?"

I shake my head. "Not really. I have a feeling I've been here before. But that's all."

I search the tables for framed photographs. None. No clues. Not one.

I go through the living room, pulling out drawers from tables. No photos. No information.

Arlene stands in the doorway with her arms crossed over her chest. "Are any memories coming back?"

"No," I reply sadly.

I see a small den at the back of the living room. I motion for Arlene to follow me there.

The room has a brown leather chair and couch, a dark wood desk . . . No photos. No books or magazines.

Arlene lingers behind me, arms still crossed as if shielding herself. "Jacob, this room . . ." Her voice trails off.

I turn to her. "What about it?"

"It . . . looks familiar to me," she says hesitantly. Her eyes move around the room, study the dark wallpaper, then move to the desk. "I think I remember being here before."

"Weird," I say. "Can you remember anything else?"

She frowns, then shakes her head. "Do you think we're crazy, Jacob? Or . . ." I can see her thinking hard. "Do you think this is some kind of a test?"

I stare hard at her. "Test?"

"Yes. I read a book once about these kids who wake up and find themselves in a strange, frightening world. They don't know where they are or what they're supposed to do. They just know they have to try and survive."

She swallows. "It turns out the kids were in some kind of science lab the whole time. It was all just a test cooked up by these scientists to see what the kids would do to stay alive."

"Weird book," I reply. "And you think —"

"Maybe that's what is happening to us," she says. "Maybe we're in a science lab, and scientists are watching us, watching our every move."

The idea gives me a chill. "Maybe," I say. "So what should we do? Just sit down and wait for them to end the experiment?"

We both know we can't do that.

What if Arlene is wrong and there are no scientists studying us?

"Hey — let's turn on the TV," Arlene cries, pointing to the small TV on a wall shelf behind me. "Hurry. Turn it on. Maybe we'll learn *something* about this place."

Arlene and I drop down side by side on the edge of the leather couch to watch.

It's a cartoon show. Two mice are chasing a dog. I was really into cartoons when I was a kid. But I've never seen this one before.

"Change the channel," Arlene says impatiently.

I grab the remote on the table beside the couch and click the channel button.

Now we're watching a game show. The contestant, a young blond-haired man, has his shirt off. I can see a large blue-and-red tattoo on his chest. He has his arm raised. A long glass tube has been inserted in the food hole in his armpit.

"What flavor is this?" the game show host asks.

Liquid flows through the tube into the man's armpit.

"Is it cherry?" he asks.

A loud buzzer rasps.

"Oh, so sorry!" the host exclaims, shaking his head. "Raspberry. Sorry, our challenge round is over. Better luck next time on *Guess the Flavor*."

"I don't believe this!" I exclaim.

I click from channel to channel. We see one weird show after another. Not one show we recognize.

On a fishing show, two men in a motorboat are pulling strange, two-headed fish from the water. On another game show, contestants are receiving jolts of electricity. The electric shocks make them jump and dance, and the audience howls with laughter.

I click the remote again, and we see a news program. A young man with a pile of sleek, wavy brown hair, wearing a dark blazer with some kind of number on the lapel, stares into the camera solemnly.

"The government has issued an alarming warning," he announces in a deep, mellow voice.

Arlene and I lean closer, listening carefully.

"Earth Geeks have landed," the news reporter continues. "Everyone should be on the lookout. Mayor-Governor Dermar has announced a state of emergency."

Arlene and I stare at each other.

Earth Geeks?

Emergency?

A grim-faced man in a black suit appears on the screen. I guess that this is Mayor-Governor Dermar.

"The Earth Geeks will not survive for long if we all are alert and do our civic duty," he booms. "Earth Geeks must go! Earth Geeks must go!"

His words send a chill down my back.

And I can't force a frightening thought from my mind.

Is this really my house?

I'm not sure anymore.

Maybe I don't live here. Maybe I don't live *anywhere*.

I turn to Arlene. I can see by her face that she has the same thought.

"Maybe *we're* the Earth Geeks!" we both say in unison.

Maybe we're the Earth Geeks — and they want to *kill* us!

click off the TV. I can't bear to hear another word.

A million questions fly into my head.

If we are the Earth Geeks, does that mean we
are no longer on Earth? Are Arlene and I on another planet? How did we get here?

Are we the only Earth Geeks? Are the two of us
all alone?

How can we hide from them if we don't know
who we are or what we're doing here?

Why do they want to kill us?

I turn to Arlene. "We've got to find some clues,
or we're doomed. Do you know where you live? Do
you have a house here?"

She shuts her eyes, concentrating, thinking
hard. "I . . . don't know. I don't remember, Jacob."

I jump to my feet. "We've got to find out some answers," I say. "If we want to survive, we've got to know what's going on."

Arlene gazes up at me from the couch. "Where should we start?"

"Right here," I tell her. "We have to search this house from top to bottom. There's got to be something here. A photo, a map, a book of some kind. Letters . . ."

"My parents must be really worried about me," Arlene says. And then she adds softly, "Wherever they are."

"Come on." I pull her to her feet, and we start searching the house.

We already checked out the living room, but we do it again.

We don't find anything.

I check out the dining room, pulling out drawers, examining shelves, even looking under the big oak table.

Nothing.

Arlene returns from the kitchen, looking very unhappy. "Some eggs in the refrigerator and a carton of milk," she reports. "Not very helpful."

"Let's check upstairs," I say.

The first room seems to be a guest room. A bed and an empty dresser. We look everywhere, even under the bed.

We search the linen closet. The upstairs bathroom.

"Is this your room?" Arlene asks as we step into the room at the end of the hall.

I gaze around at the bright blue wallpaper, the desk with a laptop computer resting on it, the bed with its pale blue bedspread.

"It . . . doesn't look familiar," I tell her. "I still think this is my house, but . . ." My voice trails off.

I see a stack of magazines on a low wooden shelf. "Maybe there's a clue in those," I say.

I race across the room. Trip on a bump in the carpet.

"Owww!" I cry out as my forehead hits the bookshelf.

I put out one hand to catch my balance and rub my aching head with the other. "Whoa."

I see a bright flash of sparkling white light.

I blink. Once. Twice.

"Hey, Arlene —" I say shakily. "I just had a flash. I just remembered something."

She narrows her eyes at me. "What is it?"

I rub my forehead. "I'm from Wisconsin," I tell her. "It just popped back into my head. I guess from bumping into the shelf. I'm from Madison, Wisconsin."

Her mouth drops open. "What else, Jacob? Think hard. Do you remember anything else?"

I shake my head. "No. That's all."

I grab the stack of magazines and shuffle through them quickly. They're all art magazines featuring artists I've never heard of. They're not written in English. They're in the squiggly, bumpy alphabet we saw in the library.

"These can't be my magazines," I say with a sigh. I drop them back onto the floor.

Arlene slumps down on the edge of the blue bedspread. She shakes her head sadly. "We're not getting anywhere."

I rub my throbbing head. I can feel a bump there. "At least I remember where I come from. That's something."

"You're ahead of me," Arlene says, lowering her head. "I don't remember anything. It's like I'm a blank. I have no past. I have no . . . identity."

I stare at her. "Maybe we're robots," I say. "I read a story once about robots whose programming got all messed up. Maybe that's us. Maybe we're some kind of computerized humanoids whose memory programs failed."

Arlene rolls her eyes. "Yeah, right," she mutters.

She pinches her arm. "It's skin, Jacob. I don't know about you, but I'm not a robot. I'm a person."

The bump on my forehead still throbs. "You're right. My robot theory is lame."

I turn to the bookshelf. "Maybe if you bump *your* head, Arlene, some of *your* memory will come back."

She frowns at me. "There's got to be a better way."

Suddenly I have an idea. "School," I blurt out.

She squints up at me from the bed. "What about it?"

"We must have school records, right? The school has to have files on us. Maybe the files are in English. Maybe they can tell us about ourselves. Come on. Let's go."

She hesitates. "You mean . . . break into the school?"

I open my mouth to answer — but I hear a sound from downstairs.

The front door closing?

Arlene jumps to her feet, her face twisted in fear. "Who is that?" she whispers.

I hear heavy footsteps. A door slams downstairs.

I tiptoe to the bedroom doorway. And listen. The hall has no windows. It's completely dark. I can't see a thing.

I hear the creak of the stairs under someone's shoes.

"He — he's coming upstairs," I whisper.

"Hide," Arlene whispers back. "Quick. The closet."

We both run to the bedroom closet.

The heavy *THUD* of footsteps reaches the landing.

I grab the doorknob, twist it, and pull.

Stuck.

The door is either stuck — or locked.

I frantically pull it again.

No. The door won't open.

We're trapped.

I spin around as a tall figure barges into the doorway.

The dark-haired man in the stained raincoat.

The frightening-looking man who chased us from the library.

He steps heavily into the room, blocking our escape. A grin spreads over his stubbled face. "Gotcha!" he cries.

He closes the door behind him. His eyes move from Arlene to me.

We stand huddled together with our backs pressed against the closet door.

My throat is choked with fear.

Who is he? What does he want?

Has he figured out our secret — that we are different? Has he come to capture us?

The man moves forward slowly. His open raincoat reveals a gray sweat suit underneath.

"Please —" Arlene whispers.

The man stops halfway across the room.

His smile fades.

"Hey — don't you recognize me?" he asks. "Why do you look so frightened?"

I stare hard at him. Should I recognize him?

"Hey, give me a break," he says. "I'm your father!"

Arlene and I both gasp.

"B-both of us?" Arlene stammers.

He nods. "Yes. I'm your dad."

My head spins. "You mean . . . Arlene and I are brother and sister?"

The man nods again. Then he studies us. "You really don't remember?"

"Our memories . . ." I say. "They're messed up."

"We hardly remember anything," Arlene adds.

He frowns. "Me too."

He steps forward to hug us.

I pull back. "Prove it," I say.

He stops in surprise. "Excuse me?"

"Prove it," I repeat. "We don't remember you. We don't even remember each other. If you're our dad, prove it."

Arlene nods agreement.

He blinks. Then he pulls off his soiled raincoat. Tugs up his sleeve. And shows us his armpit. "See? I'm like you, not like them."

"But —" I start.

"You'll have to trust me, Jakie," he says.

I gasp. "You know my nickname? You're *really* our dad?"

He wraps us in a hug. The three of us stand there with our arms tightly around each other for a long moment.

I pull back first. "Why don't we remember anything?" I ask my dad.

He shakes his head sadly. "I can't answer that. I don't know."

"Where are we? How did we get here?" I demand.

"Jakie, I don't know," he replies. He brushes back his thick black hair. "I've been struggling to remember. But it's gone . . . all gone."

He tosses his raincoat onto the bed. "I've been searching everywhere for you both," he says. "I found you at the school. But you ran away."

"I didn't know who you were," I explain.

"Is this our house? Do we have a mom?" Arlene asks, her voice trembling.

"I can't answer that, either," Dad says. "I'm sorry. I'm truly sorry. I only know one thing for sure."

"What's that?" I ask.

"The three of us — we're in terrible danger."

We make our way down to the den to talk. Dad peers out the window, making sure no one is out there. Then he pulls the drapes shut.

He drops down on the chair across from us. He leans forward tensely, his hands clenching and un-clenching in front of him. "Have you seen the TV news?" he asks.

Arlene and I nod. "We just saw it. Are we the Earth Geeks they were talking about?"

He frowns solemnly. "I guess we are."

"Why do they want to *kill* us?" Arlene asks. "How did we get here? Are we on another planet?"

Dad can't answer any of our questions. His memory is as empty as ours. I can see that every question hurts him. He wants to protect us. He wants to save us.

But he doesn't know how.

"They all want to capture the Earth Geeks," he says. "But they don't know who the Earth Geeks are. We're safe until they figure it out."

"We have to get away from here — right now!" Arlene declares. She jumps to her feet and moves toward the front door.

Dad moves quickly to stop her. "Not yet. We need to know that we can escape safely. We need to plan our escape carefully. I need time to think, Arlene."

"But . . . where do we hide in the meantime?" Arlene asks.

"We're safe here tonight," Dad replies. "Tomorrow, you should be safe at school."

"Excuse me?" I cry. "We can't go back there. We —"

"Yes. You go to school tomorrow. That's the best place to hide. Out in the open. While you're there, I'll search around. Come up with an escape plan."

He puts his arms around us again. "Don't let anyone get suspicious at school," he warns. "It's only for a day or two. Try to pass as one of them. Can you do it?"

I stare back at him. Can we do it?

Can we?

The answer, sadly, is *no*.

18

The morning passes without any problems.
It isn't easy. I don't understand the math equations, and I can't read the geography assignment.

I try to hide behind the kid in front of me, praying that Mr. Kray doesn't call on me.

My hands are cold and sweaty. I'm alert to every sound.

But no one notices me — until gym class.

As we march into the gym, I'm almost paralyzed with fear.

Will we have to change into gym clothes?

If we change, the other guys in the locker room will see that I have no food hole in my armpit. They'll know I'm an Earth Geek.

Luckily, Mr. Grody, the gym teacher, doesn't ask us to change. He lines us up against one wall of the gym. We wait as the other trelth-grade class enters. Both classes are taking gym together.

I look for Arlene. She's the very last person in her class to enter. She hangs back, hiding behind a group of other kids.

"Class against class," Mr. Grody announces. He raises a square black object, about the size of a toaster. "Who wants first blett?"

I lower my eyes to the floor. I wonder if anyone can see me trembling.

Please don't pick me, I pray. *Please, don't hand that thing to me.*

To my horror, I feel Mr. Grody's hand on my shoulder. As I look up, he slides the square object into my hand. "First blett!" he announces. "Everyone, get set!"

The black cube is light and softer than I imagined. It's kind of rubbery.

I stare at it, trying to keep my hand from trembling.

What do I do with it? What?

I look up to see all eyes on me.

Members of my team have spread themselves out behind me. Kids on the other team lean forward, hands on their knees. They are positioned over the other half of the gym.

I see Arlene, looking lost, unable to keep the fear off her face. She stares at me. I know she is wondering what I am going to do with the strange object in my hand.

Do I throw it? Do I kick it?
Do I bat something with it? Pass it to someone?
Mr. Grody blows his whistle.
Cheers ring out.
I raise the cube above my head.
I can't move. I can't breathe.
They're all waiting. All watching.
What do I do?
What?

19

I stand there frozen with the cube raised above my head.

Over the cheers and shouts, I hear Mr. Grody's whistle again.

"That's a throol, Jacob!" he shouts. "One throol!"

Another whistle blast.

I can't move. I can't think straight.

I heave the cube across the gym. I just want to get rid of it.

I gasp when I see it flying straight to Arlene.

She catches it in both hands.

Kids on her team shout angrily.

"No! No throol!"

"Harb it, Arlene! Harb it!"

I can see tears glisten on Arlene's cheeks. She

stands uncertainly, red-faced now, holding the cube in front of her.

The whistle blows again.

Mr. Grody signals for Arlene to come to him. Then he waves me forward.

His eyes move coldly from Arlene to me. "Why didn't you blett, Jacob? You had first blett."

I swallow hard. I know that everyone can see my legs trembling. My teeth actually start to chatter.

"I — I don't know the rules," I blurt out.

A mistake. A horrible mistake.

The kids circle us. They stand stiffly, eyeing us in silence. I glance at their cold, suspicious expressions.

Mr. Grody brings his face close to mine. "You don't know the rules?"

Too late to take it back. I shake my head.

"How about you?" he asks Arlene. "Do you know the rules of a game that everyone starts playing at the age of throo?"

Arlene lowers her eyes to the floor. "Not really," she confesses.

The chant begins. *"Earth Geeks . . . Earth Geeks . . . Earth Geeks . . ."*

The circle of kids grows tighter as their ugly chant grows louder. *"Earth Geeks . . . Earth Geeks . . . Earth Geeks . . ."*

Mr. Grody shakes his head. A sneer twists his

lips. "Did you really think you could get away with it? Did you really think we wouldn't find you out?"

I think about running. I turn to see the circle tightening even more. No way to break through.

No way to escape.

The circle of kids starts to move, forcing us forward. Forcing us to the gym door.

They herd us down the hall. Chanting the whole way. *"Earth Geeks . . . Earth Geeks . . . Earth Geeks . . ."*

"Let us go!" I scream.

"You're making a big mistake!" Arlene cries. "Where are you taking us?"

The chant drowns out our frightened protests.

They force us to the principal's office. The chant doesn't end until Mr. Trager takes us both into his inner office. He closes the door and bolts a latch.

His face is grim. His eyes reveal no emotion at all.

He motions with both hands for us to sit in the chairs that face his gray metal desk.

He doesn't say a word until Arlene and I are seated. Both trembling. Both gripping the chair arms so tightly, our hands are pale white.

Then he lets out his breath in a long whoosh. He leans across the desk, his hands clasped on the desktop.

"Are you the Earth Geeks?" he asks softly, calmly.

"Of course not!" I declare.

"They all made a stupid mistake," Arlene adds. "We don't know what they're talking about."

Mr. Trager raises an eyebrow suspiciously. "You don't know what Earth Geeks are?"

"Uh . . . yes. Of course we know what they are," I reply, my voice cracking. "But we're not them."

"No way," Arlene says, shaking her head. She returns his stare, trying to convince him she's not afraid.

Mr. Trager doesn't blink. He studies us coldly, thoughtfully. He picks up a pencil and taps it rapidly on the metal desktop.

"You're really not the Earth Geeks?" he asks finally. "You're telling the truth?"

I feel a spark of hope.

Maybe he is starting to believe us. Maybe if we keep lying, keep protesting, he'll let us go.

"They made a mistake," I repeat. "We're not good at sports. But that doesn't mean —"

Mr. Trager raises a hand to stop me.

I study his face. Does he believe me? Is he going to let us go?

"I'll give you a simple test," he says.

A test?

My heart sinks into the pit of my stomach. I suddenly feel sick.

"I'll ask a few really simple questions," he says, tapping the pencil more rapidly on the desk, his eyes moving back and forth between us. "It will be easy to see if you are telling the truth."

He waits, as if expecting Arlene and me to give up, to confess.

But we remain silent.

"Jacob, name the seven continents," he demands. He stops tapping, holds the pencil in the air. "I'll give you the first two — Plosia and Andrigia."

I utter a weak cry.

"Go ahead," he says in a whisper. "Name the other five."

I take a deep breath. "Well . . ."

"Jacob, do you know that there are seven continents?" he asks.

"Of course," I reply. I feel drops of sweat rolling down my burning cheeks. "Of course I know there are seven."

Mr. Trager frowns again. "Well, there aren't seven, Jacob. You just failed the test. Seven is an *Earth* number. There are gleventeen continents. We teach that in the firth grade."

"Oh," I say weakly. I slump back in the chair, feeling light-headed, dizzy, barely able to breathe.

Mr. Trager turns to Arlene. "You knew there are gleventeen continents — right?"

Arlene glances nervously at me, then back to the principal. Her chin is quivering. "Right," she says softly.

"Well, then, Arlene, I'm sure you can name our last grelve mayor-governors," Mr. Trager says, pencil poised in the air like a baton.

Arlene blinks. She doesn't say a word.

"Go ahead," the principal urges. "Name our present mayor-governor."

Arlene lowers her head. Her shoulders tremble, up and down.

Mr. Trager picks up the desk phone. He punches in three numbers. Waits a few seconds.

Then he speaks into the receiver. "Send someone over right away. We've captured the Earth Geeks."

20

As he talks into the phone, I turn and glance at the office door. Can we get out the door before he can stop us?

No.

The latch. The latch is bolted shut.

By the time I slide it open, Mr. Trager will grab us.

"Yes, yes. You may inform the mayor-governor," the principal is saying into the phone.

I turn to Arlene. I signal with my eyes.

She nods. She understands.

We both leap for the open window at the same time.

Mr. Trager cries out and drops the phone. I see him jump up from his desk chair.

But he is too late.

Arlene and I dive headfirst out the window.

75

My knees bump the window ledge on the way out. Pain shoots up my body.

I land hard on the grass. But I scramble to my feet.

I pull Arlene up, and we start to run. We jump over the low wall beyond the parking lot. And race across the playground.

I hear a clanging alarm inside the building.

Shouts. Someone waves and points at us from an upstairs classroom window.

We cut across the playground, running full speed.

"Where are we going?" Arlene cries.

"Away!" is my answer.

I let out a gasp as I hear sirens from down the street. Rising and falling, coming closer.

Sirens all around now.

Police?

Three men in dark suits run from the school. Teachers? One of them points in our direction, and they chase after us.

We cross the street, jump over a hedge, dart across someone's front yard, around the house to the back. The backyard has a picket fence around it. We hoist ourselves over the fence, our arms and legs scrambling frantically.

Into an alley. Our shoes pounding the pavement.

I gasp for breath as we turn a corner and find ourselves in another backyard.

"Whoa. Wait a sec," I cry breathlessly. I stop, panting hard, my chest heaving up and down.

Arlene wipes sweat off her forehead with one hand. Her eyes widen in fear as we hear rapid footsteps in the alley.

Where should we hide? Where?

Before we can move, a figure rushes up to us. His raincoat flaps wildly behind him. He waves frantically with both hands.

"Dad!" I cry.

"What happened?" he asks. "The sirens —"

"We were caught," I tell him. "They're coming after us."

Dad glances back to the alley. "No place to hide there. Let's go."

He pulls us toward the street. Sirens wailing nearby. Angry shouts behind us.

"We'll steal a car," Dad says, glancing up and down the street. "We'll drive away. We'll get out of here and then figure out what to do next."

Dozens of little square cars are parked up and down the street. We run up to the nearest one, a green car with bright yellow tires.

Dad tugs at the driver's door. "Locked."

The sirens grow louder, closing in on us.

We run to the next car, a black car with open windows.

Dad reaches inside, pulls the door handle, and the door swings open. He lowers himself into the driver's seat as I climb in front. Arlene dives into the back.

I slam the passenger door and turn to Dad. He's staring at the steering wheel.

It's not a wheel — it's a square panel, and it has a dozen red buttons in the center.

"Is this the wheel?" he murmurs. He lowers his head and searches for the ignition. "I should have known the cars would be strange here. I'm just not thinking clearly."

"That's okay. You can drive it! Hurry!" I urge. I peer out the window and see three black cars turn into the street, tires squealing.

"But how do you start this thing?" Dad cries.

He frantically begins jabbing at the buttons in the middle of the square panel.

We all cry out in surprise as the engine roars to life.

"Gear shift!" Dad shouts, fumbling with his right hand. "Gear shift! How do you shift? Where is it? Where?"

He can't find it. He stabs at another button on the panel.

"Whoa!" I let out a shout as the car lurches from the curb.

The tires squeal as we roar out into the street.

"No pedals!" Dad cries, gripping the square panel with both hands. "How do I slow down?"

The wail of sirens grows deafening. I poke my head out the open window — and see a line of four black cars chasing after us.

"Get going, Dad!" I shout. "They see us!"

"I — I don't know how!" Dad cries. He slams his hand on the buttons on the panel.

The car screeches to a hard stop. We slide over the pavement, tires scraping the road.

I jolt forward. My head slams against the windshield.

Dad hits more buttons. We roar forward again.

"They're catching up!" Arlene shouts. "Can't you go faster, Dad?"

Dad pounds the buttons wildly. "If only I knew how to drive this thing! It doesn't make any sense! No gas pedal! No brake!"

"They're going to catch us! They're going to catch us!" Arlene shrieks.

The sirens ring in my ears.

We're roaring over the road now. Dad struggles to keep control.

"Faster!" Arlene cries. "We're losing them!"

I see the tall redbrick wall up ahead.

My breath catches in my throat.

I try to scream. But I can't make a sound.

Dad pounds the buttons with his fist. He tries to turn the panel.

He can't control the rocketing car.

The brick wall is in front of us.

And then it fills the windshield.

I hear a horrible *CRAAAACK*, the sound of shattering glass and metal.

Then silence.

Everything goes bright red . . . then black.

21

I wake up in darkness. Try to blink it away.

Gray shapes begin to form. I see black lines up and down against dim gray light. A window.

Bars in a window.

A stone wall comes into focus. I stretch my arms. They ache. My shoulders ache.

I blink again, trying to clear my throbbing head. I clear my throat noisily. And gaze around.

It takes me a long while to realize I'm sitting on a wooden bench in a small prison cell.

In the dim light, I see a figure on the floor.

Dad?

He has a bandage on his head. Arlene is hunched on a low cot against the wall. One arm is in a heavy cast.

She blinks and stretches, opening and closing

her mouth as if testing her jaw. She raises her eyes to me. "Jacob? Are we in prison?" Her voice sounds hoarse and weak.

"Are we . . . okay?" I ask.

Dad stirs. He sits up. Feels the bandage on his head with both hands.

"The brick wall . . ." he murmurs. "The car . . ."

"Are we okay?" I repeat. My own voice sounds unfamiliar.

"My arm —" Arlene gasps. "Was it broken?" She gazes around the small cell. "Who brought us here?"

We don't have time to talk.

I hear heavy footsteps. The clang of metal. The cell door swings open.

Two black-uniformed guards step into the cell. One of them pulls Dad to his feet. His partner motions to Arlene and me. "Let's go."

"Where are we?" Dad demands. "Why did you bring us here?"

The grim-faced guards don't answer. One leads the way down a long, low-ceilinged hall. The other walks behind us, his hand resting on his gun holster.

"Is this a prison?" Dad asks.

"We didn't do anything wrong!" I tell them.

The guards don't say a word. We walk in silence, except for the thud of our shoes on the concrete floor.

It seems as if we walk for miles. My head throbs. My shoulders ache.

We turn a corner and make our way down another endless hall, closed metal doors on both sides. Finally, we stop in a yellow-tiled reception area.

One guard opens a door. "Inside," his partner orders.

"Where are you taking us?" Dad demands.

The guard shoves him in the back. Dad stumbles through the doorway. Arlene and I follow — into a wood-paneled office, bookshelves on three walls. A maroon carpet on the floor. Bright light from a large, cone-shaped ceiling fixture shines down on a dark wood desk.

The man behind the desk stands up as we enter. He appears to be about fifty or so, balding, with gray hair, a round, pale face, and steel-gray eyes. He wears a navy blue suit with some kind of red-and-yellow crest on the lapel.

"The three prisoners, Mayor-Governor," one of the guards announces.

The mayor-governor studies us as he makes his way around the large desk. "Close the door and stay at attention," he orders the guards. "These prisoners may be dangerous."

"We're *not* dangerous!" I protest.

He stares at me for a moment with his cold gray eyes. Then he turns back to the guards. "If they try to escape, kill them."

"What do you want?" I cry. "Why did you bring us here?"

He ignores my questions and steps up to my dad. He studies the bandage wrapped around Dad's head. "You need driving lessons," he says. A cruel smile spreads over his face.

"I am Mayor-Governor Dermar," he tells Dad. "Tell me your name."

"Eric Miller," Dad replies. "These are my kids, Arlene and Jacob."

We are standing awkwardly in the center of the room with the two guards at attention behind us at the door. I see four chairs in front of the desk. But the mayor-governor doesn't offer them to us.

"Why did you come here?" he asks Dad, a sneer on his lips.

"I — I don't really know," Dad stammers.

"I shall repeat the question," Dermar says coldly, through clenched teeth. "Why did you come here?"

"I don't know," Dad insists. "We don't even know where we are."

"You are lying," Dermar says softly. His pale face reddens.

"We're not lying!" Arlene screams. "We've lost our memories!"

Dermar ignores her, keeping his eyes on Dad. "Why did you come here?"

"My daughter is telling the truth," Dad replies. "All three of us don't remember. We've lost our memories."

"That story won't help you," Dermar says. He

speaks softly, but I can see his teeth grind, see his face darken even more.

"We know why you have come, Mr. Miller. We know you have the weapon."

"What weapon?" I blurt out, turning to Dad.

Dad shrugs. Beneath the heavy bandage, his eyes reveal his confusion. "I don't know anything about a weapon," he tells Dermar.

Dermar brings his face menacingly close to Dad's. "It won't help you to lie or to pretend you don't remember," he seethes. "We know you have the weapon, Mr. Miller."

"But — listen —" Dad sputters.

"We're telling the truth!" I insist.

"Where is the weapon?" the mayor-governor demands angrily. "We know you have come to destroy us."

"Destroy you?" Dad replies. "We don't even know who you are. Or where we are. Or how we got here."

Dad utters a desperate sigh. "You've got to believe us. I'm telling you the truth."

Dermar stares coldly at Dad, clenching and unclenching his jaw.

Does he believe Dad? I wonder. He's *got* to believe Dad. Dad is telling him the truth.

"Hand over the weapon now," Dermar insists.

He doesn't believe Dad at all.

"Hand over the weapon now," Dermar says

again. "If you want to save yourself and your children a lot of pain."

"Pain?" Arlene whispers.

"If you do not give me the weapon of your own free will," Dermar threatens, "I will have no choice but to torture you."

Dad's mouth drops open. But no sound comes out. The color drains from his face.

"Dad," I whisper. "Do you know what he's talking about? Do you have a weapon?"

Dad shakes his head. "No . . . I have no idea . . ."

"We will have to persuade you to talk," Dermar says softly. He signals to the guards.

They force us down a long hallway. My heart starts to race. My throat is so dry, I can't swallow.

Are they really going to *torture* us?

The guards push open a heavy, metal door.

They push us into a large, high-ceilinged room, the size of a gym.

I stare at the object in the middle of the room.

Then I start to scream.

22

A few minutes later, we are hanging by our feet. Hanging upside down, thick ropes from the ceiling tight around our ankles.

The blood rushes to my head. I feel dizzy. Sick.

My ankles throb with pain. The ropes are so tight . . . so tight.

I open my mouth and suck in deep breaths. My heart pounds so hard, my chest aches.

I am strung up in the middle, between Arlene and Dad.

My hands hang down limply. The rope sways slightly, making me swing into Arlene.

I stare down in horror.

Into the huge black cauldron beneath us.

It looks like a big pot from one of those old jungle movies with cannibals. The kind of round pot used to cook people.

Something bubbles inside it.

I stare down, shaking in terror, struggling to focus, to see what bubbles inside the cauldron.

You'll soon find out, Jacob, I tell myself.

If Dad doesn't tell them what they want, you'll soon find out what's in the pot.

"Will you hand over the weapon?" I hear Dermar's voice from somewhere behind us. "Will you spare yourselves and hand it over?"

"I — can't!" Dad groans. His face is bright red. His features are twisted in agony. "I . . . don't know . . . what you're . . . talking about."

"We don't know anything!" Arlene shrieks, her voice high with terror. "Let us go! We don't have any weapon!"

I hear Dermar sigh. "I've given you every chance."

The rope slides. The churning cauldron appears to move closer.

I realize they are lowering the ropes. Lowering us into the big pot.

Lower . . . Lower . . .

23

"**N**o — *please!*" Arlene shrieks.

"Stop! Stop it!" Dad cries.

I hear the creaking of gears as the ropes drop us lower. I grab Dad's hand as the pot appears ready to swallow us up.

And inside the pot . . .

Churning, bubbling inside the pot . . .

I see Splatters. Millions of the hairy round bugs.

Millions . . . They bubble like a thick, dark stew. Grunting and groaning, the Splatters churn in the big pot.

My hands dip into the cauldron. The Splatters swarm over them. Over my hands and wrists. Sticky and warm, their bristly black hair prickling my skin.

They stick to my hands, my arms.

Lower . . .

88

They swarm over my shoulders.

"Oh . . . hellllp," I hear Arlene moan. "This is soooo sick. . . ."

Lower . . .

I try to whistle. I remember that whistling makes the Splatters weak.

But my breath catches in my throat.

The hairy, bubble-shaped creatures stick to me. Climb over me. Grunting as they swarm.

We're going to drown, I realize.

We're going to drown in Splatter bugs.

Lower . . .

My head hits the side of the pot, then sinks inside.

I open my mouth to try whistling again — and a Splatter rolls onto my tongue.

The Splatters are in my hair now. They cling to my face.

I shut my eyes —

— and hear them!

Yes.

They're speaking to me.

Silently.

I can read their thoughts! I realize.

This is amazing!

"We . . . won't . . . hurt . . . you." Their words ring in my mind.

Am I going crazy? I wonder. Am I just dreaming this, *hoping* this? Or are they really communicating with me?

I sink lower. . . .

My shoulders slip into the churning, fat insects.

I can't see Dad or Arlene now. My head is buried in the sticky, hairy bugs.

"We . . . won't . . . hurt . . . you. Pretend to cooperate . . . with Dermar. . . ."

I *can* hear their voices in my mind. I really can!

Should I trust them?

Do I have a choice?

"Dad —" I try to call out. I wonder if he can hear them too.

But I can't make a sound. I'm choking in the thick sea of Splatters. They crawl over my forehead, onto my eyelids, into my ears.

"Pretend . . . to cooperate . . . with Dermar."

But it's too late, I think.

I feel the ropes loosen and slide off my ankles.

I plunge deeper into the sticky, fat insects.

I'm drowning, I realize.

I can't breathe . . . can't breathe at all.

24

I fall into the sticky warmth. So black ... so black now ... darker than the darkest night.

I open my mouth, struggling to gasp in air. But Splatters pour onto my tongue.

Their low, short grunts fill my ears.

My chest aches.

Can't breathe ... can't breathe.

And then from somewhere far away, I hear Dad's voice. "Okay! I'll give it to you!"

Silence.

Then Dad again. "Let us out! I'll give you the weapon!"

"Dad —" I whisper. "Do you really have a weapon?"

"No," he replies. "I — I'm only stalling."

I feel the cauldron start to tilt.

I'm sliding . . . sliding with the bugs. Tumbling over them, through them.

We tilt harder.

Someone is tilting the whole pot, tilting us out.

My head bobs up from the thick blanket of insects. I suck in a deep, cool breath.

It feels so good. Panting like a dog, I start breathing again.

We all topple out of the cauldron. I land hard on my back on the floor.

All three of us sprawl on the floor, covered in the sticky bugs.

I brush them from my eyes. Slap them from my hair. I try to whistle, but my mouth is too dry.

I see Arlene brushing Splatters off her cast. Pulling them from her ears. She plucks a fat, hairy one off her tongue.

I pull them out from under my shirt. They make a soft *POP* as I tug them off my chest.

I roll onto my side. Gaze at Dad.

"What are you going to do?" I whisper. "Were you telling the truth about the weapon? Do you have one?"

Dad sits up and stares back at me. "No. I don't know anything about a weapon," he whispers.

I turn to see the cauldron tilt onto its side. An avalanche of Splatters pours out. Like an ocean wave, the millions of grunting bugs roll over the floor.

Dermar steps forward, trailed by his two guards.

He reaches out his hand. "The weapon — now!" he demands.

Arlene and I stare at Dad. What is he going to do?

We don't have a chance to find out.

Dermar lets out a scream as the wave of Splatters attacks him.

The fat, bubble-shaped bugs swarm over Dermar and his guards.

The insects cover the three men quickly. In seconds, I cannot see their faces, their uniforms.

Dermar and his guards collapse under the weight of the bugs. And vanish from view.

And then, as I stare in amazement, I see Dermar stagger to his feet. Covered in the sticky insects, Dermar and the guards rise up. They stumble forward for a few steps.

Turn. And run.

Splatters fall off them as they bolt for the door — and disappear outside.

Dad, Arlene, and I stand in a row, still breathing hard, still frozen in shock.

My teeth chatter. My legs prickle and itch.

"We're . . . okay," Arlene whispers uncertainly. "They're . . . gone."

I pull a Splatter off the back of my neck and drop it to the floor.

"Maybe we can get out of here," Dad says, his voice hoarse and dry.

"But — where can we go?" I ask.

Before anyone can answer, the Splatters rise up.

I see them roll around, like a wave pulling back from the shore.

They turn to face us.

They swarm over each other, climbing, rising up to block our way.

They're going to attack *us* now, I realize.

We're . . . doomed.

25

We are trapped. The Splatters block the way to the door.

They climb over each other, building a pyramid. A pyramid taller than we are.

Dad, Arlene, and I inch away. My legs are trembling now. My teeth are still chattering.

My back hits the wall.

The pyramid of insects slides toward us over the floor.

Arlene presses her hand against the side of her face.

I take a deep breath and prepare for them to swarm over us.

But to my surprise, the seething, churning pyramid stops a few feet in front of us.

And the Splatter at the very top speaks to us — silently — speaks to us in our minds.

"Do not be afraid." I hear his words so clearly, even though he doesn't make a sound.

"I am Grolff, the appointed leader," he says. "We brought you here from Earth. We erased your memories. We wanted to make sure you had the weapon."

"Weapon?" Dad cries. "What weapon?"

"The weapon that will allow us to destroy them," Grolff replies.

"You want to destroy those people?" Dad asks. "Why?"

"They treat us like *bugs*!" Grolff declares angrily. "We are superior to them in every way. We have superior intelligence. We are smarter than they will ever be. But because of our looks, they treat us like insects!"

I watch Grolff pulsing on top of the living pyramid of Splatters. I hear his words ring in my mind — and I feel his intense anger.

"They kill us for no reason!" Grolff cries. "They smack us between their hands for their own amusement. They take our lives daily, and they think it's funny. They kill us and *laugh*!"

I shut my eyes. His anger is making my head hurt.

When I open them again, Grolff is still pulsing above us at the top of the Splatters pyramid.

"You will hand over the weapon now," I hear him say to Dad. "You have brought from Earth the weapon that will put us in charge and finally put an end to all the slaughter."

"But — what weapon?" Dad demands. "I swear. I really don't know what you're talking about."

"Your wristwatch," Grolff replies. "Give it to us — now."

"Huh?" Dad raises his wrist and gapes at his watch. "My watch? How can that possibly help you?"

"We planted a powerful bomb in it," Grolff explains. "Back on Earth. Before we brought you here. Before we erased your memories. We planted a bomb in your wristwatch."

Dad stares at the watch. "But — but —" he sputters.

"We planted it where our enemies would never think of looking," Grolff says.

Dad stares at the watch. His whole arm starts to tremble.

"Just hand it to us," Grolff insists. "And you will be a hero to all of us. We will always remember you. We will always remember you as heroes. Hand us the watch, and we will finally be free. We will finally be able to defeat the evil ones, our enemies."

Dad raises his wrist. He reaches for the watch.

"Thank you for your bravery," Grolff says. "Our thanks go out to all three of you."

The tall, sticky pyramid of Splatters seethes

and bubbles with excitement. A shrill chattering sound rings out.

Dad pulls off the watch. He examines it one more time. Then he holds it out to Grolff.

Dad gasps as I grab the watch from his hand.

I move quickly. I don't give anyone a chance to react.

I smash the watch against the wall.

Smash it. Smash it until the crystal shatters.

Then I smash it again.

"Jacob — no!" Dad gasps. "Why did you do that? Why?"

26

'm breathing hard. My heart thuds like a jackhammer against my chest.

My hand trembles as I hold up the broken wristwatch.

It starts to shake in my hand.

It shakes harder.

A high squeal pours out of it.

"You set off the alarm!" Grolff shrieks. "Nooooooo! Turn it off! Turn off the alarm! You *fooooool!*"

The squeal is deafening, higher and louder than any siren.

I ignore Grolff's frantic cries of protest. I let the squealing watch fall to the floor, and I press my hands over my ears.

Arlene and Dad frantically cover their ears.

But the sound is too shrill, too loud. I can't keep it out.

It sends a stab of pain through my head.

I press my hands harder over my ears.

Louder ... The sound rises, blaring higher, harder.

I turn and see the Splatters begin to pop.

POP POP POP POP.

Hundreds of them popping at once, splattering yellow goo into the air.

The shrill squeal is making the Splatters explode.

Each *POP* sends another yellow spurt flying.

In seconds, the floor is littered with the flat, hairy bodies of the dead Splatter bugs. The bodies rest in thick puddles of yellow goo.

"Hey!" I cry out as the yellow liquid splashes into my face. I cover my eyes, try to wipe the hot goo off my skin.

POPOPOPOP.

The Splatters are dying. Exploding. Splattering.

The pyramid collapses.

Waves of yellow goo splash onto Dad, Arlene, and me. The thick liquid spreads like a lake over the floor.

It takes only a few minutes.

The Splatters all explode.

Silence now. The sound of popping bodies has stopped.

The squeal from the watch begins to fade.

I wipe a thick splotch of yellow goo from my forehead. My hands are stained and sticky. My clothing is drenched.

I step over the watch. Dad and Arlene move unsteadily away from the wall.

We're all drenched and dazed and dizzy.

The squeal from the watch has stopped completely, but my ears still ring.

We stumble toward the door. No one speaks.

The only sound is the *CRUNCH* of Splatter bodies under our shoes.

We slip and slide to the door.

"Why?" Dad asks in a whisper. "Why, Jakie? I was going to give the watch to the Splatters. Why did you smash it and set off the alarm?"

"I knew they were evil," I explain. "I could hear Grolff's voice in my mind. Then, suddenly, I could read his thoughts too. After we gave them the watch, they planned to splatter *us!*"

"Maybe we can sneak out of here," Dad whispers. "Maybe we can find a place to hide. A place where we can think."

He reaches for the door. But it swings open before he can touch it.

Dermar bursts in, followed by four uniformed guards. "Where do you think *you're* going?" he booms.

27

"**O**hhhh." A horrified moan escapes my throat.

I sink back.

My legs tremble. I suddenly feel dizzy and weak.

Arlene grabs my hand. Her fingers are ice-cold.

A sneer crosses Dermar's lips as he gazes at the carpet of dead Splatter bodies and yellow goo. He studies the horrifying scene for a few seconds. Then he turns his strange gray eyes back on us.

"You're not going anywhere," he says, "until we have a celebration!"

We gape at him in shock. My mouth drops open. I struggle to catch my breath.

"A celebration?" Arlene chokes out.

Dermar nods. A smile spreads over his face.

"You have destroyed our enemies by setting off that alarm," he says.

The four guards let out a cheer. "You are national heroes!" one of them declares.

"Heroes? Us?" I blurt out.

"Heroes!" the other guards agree.

"The Splatters were evil," Dermar explains. "We were never safe while they were here. They were always plotting to take over. We tried to make peace with them. But they were always plotting to destroy us."

Dermar brushes a glob of yellow goo off Dad's shoulder. He shakes Dad's hand. Then he gleefully shakes hands with Arlene and me.

"The Splatters brought Earth Geek after Earth Geek here to destroy us," he continues. "They planted weapons on the Earth Geeks and erased their memories. That's why we were so eager to find you. We knew they had planted some kind of bomb on you Geeks."

"Uh, sir?" I say. "We don't really like to be called Geeks. It's an insult back on Earth."

Dermar's face reddens. "Oh. I'm terribly sorry," he says. "On our planet, it's a compliment. I had no idea. I never meant to insult you."

He motions to the door. "Come. Let's get you some fresh clothes. And then we will celebrate. We will have a grand celebration in the ballroom and invite everyone to toast our triumph and salute you for your courage."

I have a big smile on my face as I follow Dermar down the hall.

Dad and Arlene are smiling too.

We're feeling pretty good about ourselves.

We're feeling very relieved.

We're feeling like heroes.

We have no idea that the *worst* news is still to come.

28

The celebration goes on for two days.

Thousands of happy people come to the grand ballroom in the mayor-governor's residence. They eat and drink and dance and pay tribute to us.

A hundred different bands play. People dance until they drop — strange dances I've never seen before.

Endless food tables are emptied by the hungry partygoers — and then filled again.

I've never seen so much food and so much champagne flowing down people's armpits!

Dad, Arlene, and I wear black-and-gold uniforms just like Dermar's.

Mine is itchy and kind of tight. But it's better than my goo-stained jeans and T-shirt.

We party and dance and eat along with everyone else. I've never been to a wild party like this. I can't believe it's in our honor!

Every few hours, Dermar stops the music and gets everyone quiet so he can make a speech. In his speeches, he praises us and tells everyone how brave we were in defeating the Splatters. He tells everyone that I was the bravest and wisest of all since I was the one who smashed the watch and set off the alarm.

Once his speech ends, the music starts up again, and the party begins as if it never ended.

After the second day, the party still goes strong. But we are exhausted.

With our arms wearily around each other's shoulders, we find Dermar sitting in a corner. He is stuffing chocolate cake into his armpit.

Two guards stand at his sides. One holds his drink. The other holds a plate with another slice of chocolate cake.

"Enjoying the party?" Dermar asks. His armpit makes sucking sounds as it finishes off the cake. He lowers his arm.

"It's awesome!" I reply.

Arlene yawns. "Awesome," she repeats wearily.

"It's a wonderful party, Dermar," Dad says. "We want to thank you. We will never forget it."

"Of course you won't," Dermar replies, reaching for the other slice of cake.

"We have a favor to ask now," Dad says.

Dermar shoves a hunk of cake into his armpit. "A favor?" he asks over the loud chewing sounds.

Dad nods. "My kids and I are very homesick. We would like to return to Earth now."

Dermar gazes up at him. A frown creases his forehead. "Return to Earth?" He lowers his arm.

"Yes," Dad says. "We are ready to go home."

Dermar's frown deepens. "I'm sorry," he says softly. "I'm afraid I have bad news for you."

"B-bad news?" I stammer.

"We can't send you home," he says. "We don't have space travel."

"But — but how did we get here?" I cry.

"The Splatters had space travel. They were the only ones who knew how to bring you here. They were a little ahead of us in that area."

"But we *have* to get home!" Arlene cries.

Dermar climbs to his feet. He places a hand on Arlene's shoulder. "Don't worry," he says. "We will make you a home here."

He turns to Dad. "We have surgeons who can build eating tubes in your armpits," Dermar says. "That way, you will feel like one of us."

Dermar shoves us toward the door. "Come," he says. "I shall take you to the surgeons now."

107

29

One of the guards stops Dermar. "I have an idea," he says. "Remember Crazy Old Phil? He has been experimenting with a spaceship."

Dermar shakes his head. "Too dangerous," he murmurs. "We're not trusting them to Crazy Old Phil. We can't have our national heroes risking their lives."

"But can his spaceship take us back to Earth?" I ask. "We appreciate your kindness. But we really want to go home."

"Phil is brilliant but crazy," Dermar says. "Nothing he builds ever works. I don't think you'll be safe in his spaceship."

"But it's worth a try!" I insist.

Dad and Arlene agree.

"Please, let us go see it," Dad pleads. "Let's see if Phil thinks he can send us home."

Dermar shrugs. "You are national heroes," he says. "If you want to risk your lives, I cannot say no. But I hope you do not become *dead* national heroes."

Me too, I think, swallowing hard. Me too.

Phil is a skinny little guy with stick arms and legs and a long, skinny head. The way he leans over as he talks, rubbing his slender hands together, makes me think he looks more like a grasshopper than a human.

He has bushy brown hair that stands straight up on his head and tiny green eyes that dart from side to side. And he often opens his mouth wide in a whinnying horse laugh that reveals a mouthful of long, crooked teeth.

For some reason, even though he works outdoors in his backyard, Phil wears a long white cook's apron on top of his overalls and yellow flannel shirt.

"What do you know. What do you know," he keeps repeating as Dad, Arlene, and I check out his spaceship.

It's enormous, rising up in the center of his yard, twice as tall as the flagpole next to the fence. It's made of some kind of shiny metal and is shaped like a jet plane, only standing on its tail.

"What do you know. What do you know," Phil murmurs. He stops to tighten a bolt near the rocket door.

"Will it fly?" Dad asks. "Have you tested it? Will it take us to Earth?"

Phil rubs his pointy chin. "Only one way to test it," he drawls in his soft, scratchy voice.

"Is it safe?" Arlene asks.

Phil nods. "It should be safe. The Splatters weren't that far ahead of us. They weren't as smart as they thought. I used their plans. And made some improvements. This ship should take you safely to Earth."

Dad, Arlene, and I huddle together by the fence.

We know we have no choice. We don't want to stay here. We don't want food holes drilled into our armpits.

We want to go home.

We have to try Phil's spaceship.

The next day, a thousand people pour into Phil's backyard to see us off.

Dermar stands on a small platform and gives another speech. He wishes us a safe flight.

"Safe flight!" the thousand people shout.

Then, as they all cheer us on, Phil pulls open the spaceship hatch.

I lead the way up a metal gangplank.

We step into the spaceship and take our places at the control panel. We strap ourselves in the way Phil instructed the previous day.

The control panel flashes and clicks and beeps.

The sound of the cheering crowd vanishes as the spaceship hatch is shut from outside.

I grip the arms of my cockpit chair tightly. "Are we going to be okay?" I ask in a whisper.

"Phil says the ship is safe," Dad replies. "We have to trust Phil. He says he'll get us to Earth."

Dad's words are brave, but I see his chin quiver. He stares straight ahead at the blinking control panel.

We wait for Phil to hit an outside control that will blast us into space.

And we wait.

And wait.

What's happening? I wonder. What is taking so long?

And then I hear a low rumbling sound.

The rumbling grows into a roar.

The spaceship starts to shake. Harder. Harder.

And then it blows up.

30

I shut my eyes. Wait for the crushing pain.
Wait for the endless darkness.

But no.

The spaceship rumbles around me. I open my eyes and see the lights flashing on the control panel.

Dad and Arlene are smiling.

"Not an explosion," I murmur. I grin back at them. "I thought the spaceship blew up."

"Me too," Dad admits. "It was just the takeoff."

"We're on our way!" Arlene cries happily. "And if Phil did everything right, we should be home in no time."

Yesterday, Phil told us he used a space-time continuum system. I don't really understand it. But it means that we should arrive back on Earth almost before we left.

I gaze at the blinking controls and relax a little.

A hard jolt makes all three of us cry out.

The spaceship rocks hard, shaking and cracking.

My head jerks forward. Then I feel my whole body pulled back.

We sit in silence for a few seconds.

"I . . . I think we landed," Dad murmurs.

The hatch slides open.

Bright sunlight pours into the spaceship.

"Is it *our* sun?" Arlene asks, unstrapping herself. "Are we really back on Earth?"

My heart pounds as I follow Dad and Arlene off the spaceship. I gaze out at a sun-drenched neighborhood. A soft breeze flutters the trees.

I'm so happy, I want to kiss the ground!

Grass. Beautiful green grass. On beautiful green lawns.

And under a blue sky — houses. Houses in a row behind trees and hedges. Normal houses.

A normal neighborhood.

We don't know what town we're in. Or in what state or what country.

But we're so happy, all three of us go skipping down the street arm in arm.

We stop when we come to a man and a woman pulling up weeds in a front yard.

"Good morning!" I cry happily to them.

"Beautiful day, isn't it!" Dad adds, grinning.

The man and woman smile back at us.

113

Then they pull off their heads and raise them high in the air.

I gape in horror as scaly purple lizard heads poke up from their open necks.

"Yes, it's a beautiful day," one lizard head replies. "Are you from around here?"

About the Author

R.L. Stine is the most popular author in America. He is the creator of the *Goosebumps, Give Yourself Goosebumps, Fear Street,* and *Ghosts of Fear Street* series, among other popular books. He has written over 250 scary novels for kids. Bob lives in New York City with his wife, Jane, teenage son, Matt, and dog, Nadine.